SOPHIE and the HEIDELBERG CAT

Andrew Wilson

ILLUSTRATIONS BY
Helena Perez Garcia

:: CROSSWAY ®

WHEATON, ILLINOIS

Sophie and the Heidelberg Cat
Copyright © 2019 by Andrew Wilson
Illustrations © 2019 Crossway

Published by Crossway
 1300 Crescent Street
 Wheaton, Illinois 60187

Illustrations and book design: Helena Perez Garcia
Cover design: Helena Perez Garcia
First printing 2019
Printed in China
ISBN: 978-1-4335-6418-5

Library of Congress Cataloging-in-Publication Data

Names: Wilson, Andrew, 1978– author. | Perez Garcia/ Helena, illustrator.
Title: Sophie and the Heidelberg cat / Andrew Wilson ; illustrated by Helena Perez Garcia.
Description: Wheaton, Illinois : Crossway, 2019. | Summary: Grace, the talking cat next door, helps a guilty Sophie understand that even though everyone disobeys God, hope can be found in Jesus's sacrifice, promises, and protection.
Identifiers: LCCN 2018055381 | ISBN 9781433564185 (hc)
Subjects: | CYAC: Stories in rhyme. | Hope—Fiction. | Christian life—Fiction. | Cats—Fiction.
Classification: LCC PZ8.3.W687 So 2019 | DDC [E]—dc23
LC record available at https://lccn.loc.gov/2018055381

Crossway is a publishing ministry of Good News Publishers.
RRD   29 28 27 26 25 24 23 22 21 20 19
15 14 13 12 11 10 9 8 7 6 5 4 3 2 1

For Zeke, Anna, and Sam

Sophie is crying. Her sister Michaela
has broken her dollhouse, and nobody cares.
To make matters worse, she's pushed over her sister,
then yelled at her parents, and stormed up the stairs.

She looks out the window and sees, on the chimney,
the cat from the Heidelbergs' house, next door.
She stares at it, when, to her utter amazement,
it suddenly asks her, "You're crying. What for?"

9

Sophie is very surprised (but she knows
that you cannot tell lies to a talking cat).
"Michaela just broke my new dollhouse," she says.
"So I gave her a shove, and I knocked her down flat.

Then I screamed at my parents, and ran to my room,
and now I feel guilty for doing all that.
In fact, I feel worse about me than the dollhouse."
"What do you mean?" asks the Heidelberg cat.

"Well," Sophie whispers, "I've upset Michaela,
I've upset my Mom, and I've upset my Dad.
And worst of all, I've even upset God!
And the Bible says that means I'm really bad."

The cat puts its paws on the windowsill, grins,
and says, "Sophie, let's go for a rooftop walk."
Quick as a flash, Sophie climbs out the window.
(She knows you say yes to a cat that can talk.)

Scrambling up tiles and walking down roofs,

they peer into houses and gardens, and chat.

(The birds in the skies raise their eyes in surprise

at a girl on the roof with a talking cat.)

14

"Right," says the cat, "you just mentioned the Bible.
So what do you think it is trying to say?"
"Easy," says Sophie. "It's trying to tell us
how we can please God, and be kind, and obey.

Be bold like King David, be brave like Queen Esther,
and do what God tells you, no matter how scary.
Don't fight him, like Pharaoh, or trick him, like Judas.
Be patient, like Paul, and respectful, like Mary."

The cat looks at Sophie. "And are you?" it asks.

"Not really," says Sophie, "at least, not for long.

"That's why I was crying before. It's so hard

to be good all the time, and it always goes wrong."

"Aha," says the cat. "Let me tell you a secret:
There's no one who can. Not your Mom or your Dad,
your friends or your neighbors. And even your teacher,
when no one can see, is surprisingly bad.

Look round the street. Mrs. Gubbins is rude.

The Macintosh children are always in fights.

The pastor gets angry, the shopkeeper's proud,

and the Joneses have horrible quarrels at night."

Sophie looks puzzled. "That's awful," she says.

"What hope is there, if things are really like that?"

She sits on a chimney and stares at the sky.

"I'm so glad you asked," says the Heidelberg cat.

"The Bible tells stories of hundreds of people,

and all of them disobey God . . . except one.

So hope doesn't come from the good things we do.

It comes as a gift, from what Jesus has done.

21

"You've trusted in him, so he's paid for your sins,
and thrown them all into the depths of the sea.
By rising again, he has broken the power
of death, and the devil, and let you go free.

"He watches your life. He makes all things work out.
He helps you make choices. He tells you what's true.
He promises you'll live forever with him.
And that's why the hope comes from him, not from you."

Sophie sits still, to make sure the cat's finished.

She has enough questions to talk for a week.

(But knows very well, as I'm sure you do too,

that you always leave time for a cat that can speak.)

"I'd better go home," Sophie finally says.
"And tell them I'm sorry. But thanks for the talk.
I'm so looking forward to telling my friends
that I spoke to a cat, and we went for a walk."

"One other thing you should know," says the cat,
as it silently crosses the tiles on all fours.
"The best and most comforting news in the world
is that I am not mine, and you are not yours."

Sophie is shocked. "What on earth do you mean?"

"Well, look at the tag on my neck," says the cat.

"It tells you my name, then it tells you my owners.

The Heidelbergs bought me, I'm theirs, and that's that.

27

"The same goes for you. You've been rescued by Jesus,

so he is your Master from now till you die.

He'll love you, protect you, and never neglect you—

but you're not your own, Sophie. Neither am I."

At last they arrive, right outside Sophie's window.

She clambers back in with her hand on the slat.

"When will I see you again?" Sophie asks.

"I'm not sure you will," says the Heidelberg cat.

"But to help you remember our first conversation,

I'll give you my tag, with my name. Just in case."

With that, it goes back to the Heidelbergs' chimney.

Sophie looks down at the tag. It says:

"Grace."

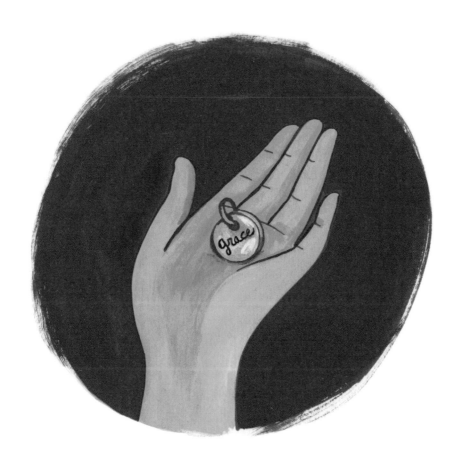

Note to Parents:

This book is based on the Heidelberg Catechism, a Christian document that was written in Germany in 1563. It takes the form of a series of questions and answers on Christian belief, based mostly around the Apostles' Creed, the Ten Commandments, and the Lord's Prayer. Its most famous section comes at the very beginning, and this is the basis for Sophie's conversation with the Heidelberg cat:

Q1. What is your only comfort in life and in death?
A1. That I am not my own, but belong—body and soul, in life and in death—to my faithful Savior, Jesus Christ. He has fully paid for all my sins with his precious blood, and has set me free from the tyranny of the devil. He also watches over me in such a way that not a hair can fall from my head without the will of my Father in heaven; in fact, all things must work together for my salvation. Because I belong to him, Christ, by his Holy Spirit, assures me of eternal life and makes me wholeheartedly willing and ready from now on to live for him.